WILD VOICES

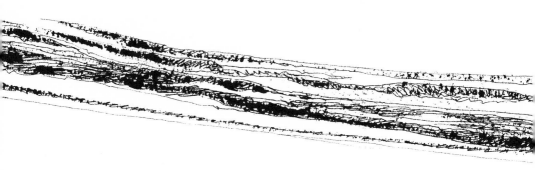

DREW NELSON

WILD VOICES

ILLUSTRATED BY
JOHN SCHOENHERR

PHILOMEL BOOKS · NEW YORK

This is for my father, who first took me to wild places.
For my brother, who takes me there still.
For my wife, Vaunda, whose boundless love, care, and
unwavering belief makes the work possible.

But mostly this is for all the animals,
wild and not, whose lives so enrich mine.
—D.N.

For the inhabitants of wilderness.
—J.S.

Text copyright © 1991 by Drew Nelson
Illustrations copyright © 1991 by John Schoenherr
Published by Philomel Books,
a division of The Putnam & Grosset Book Group,
200 Madison Avenue, New York, NY 10016
Published simultaneously in Canada. All rights reserved.
Book design by Jean Weiss

Library of Congress Cataloging-in-Publication Data
Nelson, Drew, 1952-
Wild Voices/by Drew Nelson; illustrations by John Schoenherr.
p.   cm.
Summary: Relates a winter story of two farm dogs and each of five wild
animals: a fox, a lynx, a horse, a wolf, and a puma.
ISBN: 0-399-21798-3.
1. Animals—Juvenile fiction.   1. Animals—Fiction.   2. Winter—Fiction.
I. Schoenherr, John, ill.   II. Title.
PZ10.3.N225Fo   1991   90-19717 CIP AC
[Fic]—dc20

First Impression

CONTENTS

FOXTROT

The night wind was very cold, blowing by the small hole halfway up the hillside in the small hidden valley. Even though the hole was screened by a thick thatch of brown honeysuckle vines, the wind going by made a quiet sound like a low moan. Almost as soon as it was made, the sound was carried away and then faded before it could be blown down to the farm on the flatlands below.

February snow wrapped the valley in a cloak of frost and covered the house and barn on the flatlands like a thick goose-down blanket. Its stark whiteness reflected moonlight and starlight in eerie patterns that changed the country landscape into a strange and foreign place.

The sound of the wind awakened Fox from a deep sleep. She was curled into a tight ball of fox fur that helped keep her warm as she slept. All four feet were tucked together and she pillowed her head on them. Her tail was wrapped tightly over her sharp muzzle like a thickly furred scarf. Without moving, Fox opened her eyes and glanced around to make sure she was still safe in her den. Only then did she lift her ears to listen hard for any sound of danger that could have awakened her. There was only the wind.

If there had been danger, any tiny movement may have given her away and told a farm dog, or maybe a lynx, just where she was. Satisfied that she was safe, Fox uncurled, yawned, and stretched her long, slender, delicately muscled body. She padded down the short sloping entryway of her den and poked her muzzle through the honeysuckle vines. As she smelled the air, its bitter chill froze the moisture on her nose. Fox pulled her muzzle in through the leafless vines and rubbed it with her paw.

It was much warmer in her den because her mother had taught her to always dig the entryway with a little slope upward. Then, when the bitter winter winds blew hard and cold, the heat from her body would stay trapped in the little den she had made at the upper end of the tunnel.

Fox sat down at the lower end of the tunnel and wrapped her tail close around her feet against the cold. Soon enough she would have to leave the warmth and safety of her den. Then her feet would stay cold until she returned.

She looked out through the honeysuckle at the moon-washed countryside. This was her domain. To-night she would hunt it because she had already eaten the last of her previous kill. Tonight she would move across her valley, like a shadow of death, looking for prey.

Jim, the big mongrel farm dog, slept in the barn where he could guard the animals his Man tended. Jim didn't worry much about the cows in the barn. They could take care of themselves because there weren't any wild animals big enough to trouble them. The grown sheep could also defend themselves against all of the predators that stalked the farm, except for the lynx, but the wild cat hardly ever came down to the farm and its dangers.

It was only when food ran short where he lived, high up in the hill country above the farm, that the short-tailed lynx would dare steal down to the farmland on his large, whisper-soft feet. Even then, the lynx preferred to take a chicken or a lamb or a calf. These the lynx could prey upon without fear of the flying hooves of a mature animal that could break his leg or crush his skull. Any injury that hampered the lynx's hunting ability could mean death by starvation.

The lynx also knew that Jim watched over the animals on the farm. Jim had discovered the lynx prowling near the henhouse one night and had driven him off. Jim was a fierce fighter and his loud barking brought the Man and his gun. The lynx had seen enough of Men to know that they could hurt him without getting close enough to even touch him. A meager diet of mice, when the lynx could find enough of them to survive on, was better than risking the dangers of the farm.

What worried Jim more than the lynx were the smaller predators that would sneak onto the farm and carry off one of the animals he guarded. The weasel could easily fit through the gaps in the wooden floor of the henhouse and take a fat young chicken, or several chicks. If the chickens made a big fuss, the weasel might even be overcome by the thrill of the hunt and kill more than he could carry off or eat.

The big blacksnake that lived under the barn worried Jim, too. It did a good job of keeping mice and rats out of the barn, but sometimes it would eat a chick or some hen's eggs and that would make Jim's Man angry. Jim always tried to keep watch on the henhouse when the blacksnake was moving under the barn floor.

What worried Jim most was the fox. She was big enough to carry off a newborn lamb, and she was small enough to get into the henhouse and take a full-grown chicken. February was lambing time on Jim's farm and he would dream about the fox carrying off all the new lambs. In his dream, Jim would chase the fox until his tongue hung out of his mouth. The fox would dance tantalizingly just out of his reach. Then she would disappear, and Jim knew she was back at his barn taking another lamb.

Jim dreamt his fox dream tonight, and he whimpered with frustration in his sleep. Jim's feet kicked and his skin twitched. He growled at the dancing fox and his hackles stood on end. Jim jumped at the dream fox and the movement awakened him.

He bounced to his feet and growled a deep, fierce rumble. All of the sheep in the pen moved nervously to the far wall. They baaaed soft baaas and stamped their hooves. Jim's growl had frightened them. They moved back from the wall when Jim sat down and began to lick the pads of his front paw.

Fox froze in her tracks.

She was looking for mice, moving silently along a fence line that ran between her valley and the upper fields of the farm, when she heard it.

The wind carried it in, a low menacing dog growl.

Fox very, very slowly crouched exactly where she was. Every nerve in her body quivered. Her ears twitched in one direction, then another, trying to find the source of the sound. She smelled the air deeply, but there was only the scent of the farm below and the woods above. Faintly she smelled the dangers of dog and lynx, but they were too far off to threaten.

Fox stayed motionless for a long time, until she was sure there was no danger. She didn't want to make the mistake of moving too soon just because she didn't see or smell anything right away. Her ears and nose and eyes were her survival tools, but stealth was her ally.

More than once, keeping very, very still had saved her from grave trouble.

The last time had been after she chased a squirrel up the long, low-hanging branch of an elm tree she had been able to jump up on. The squirrel reached his nest in the tree before she caught him, but as she started down she caught sight of the lynx. He was sneaking along, smelling the air, looking for his own dinner.

Fox crouched on the tree limb near where it joined the trunk and stayed as still as a stone. The lynx, who could climb far better than Fox ever could, never saw her. Her scent was carried away above him so he never even smelled her. She had watched death stalk by under that elm tree and had been saved by knowing when *not* to run.

Now, sure that she was safe, she continued her hunt along the fence line. She moved slowly, muzzle low, ears cocked forward, listening for the scratching sound of a mouse running through its tunnel under the snow. During the long, cold hours she'd been out, Fox had caught and eaten only three.

She stopped when she heard it, one forepaw raised delicately. Turning her head from side to side, she located exactly where the mouse was—so close to a sprig of mountain columbine that the winter-dried leaves trembled. She crouched, then pounced in a high arc. When her front paws landed, they hit the mouse and stunned it. Before the mouse could recover, fox dug it out of the snow, broke its neck, and swallowed it.

That was enough. She'd had a lucky night mousing and this last morsel had quieted her hunger. She headed back toward her den, checking her territory during the return trip.

Fox's quick-stepping gait brought her to the den long before the sun rose. She looped the hillside of her den to make sure there was no danger, no predator like the lynx to see where she lived, and then crawled through the vines into her tunnel. She paused just inside to chew and lick the snow from between her toes and the pads of her feet, and walked up the passageway to her den room.

She groomed her tail, pulling out a burr that had stuck there during her hunt, then curled up, drew her feet together for a pillow, and covered her face with her tail.

Fox listened for a few minutes to the faraway sounds of the night, but soon fell into a deep, safe sleep.

Jim was up with the dawn, walking the farm with his Man while he did the chores. After a while, Jim caught a scent on the air and followed it out of the barn into the frozen yard. One interesting smell led him to another, and another, and another, until Jim was drawn out into the fields.

Snuffling along the upper fence line, Jim came across the faint cold scent of fox. He trailed the fading wildness and stopped here and there along the way to mark the trail with his own scent. Jim considered this upper part of the farm to be his territory and his scent would carry that message to the fox.

After a while, Jim lost Fox's scent in the woods. By then his feet were nearly frozen, and he headed back to the warmth of his straw bed in the barn. This night, Fox had escaped Jim's wrath.

The moon was on the wane when Fox next hunted for her dinner. If she had found something larger than mice the night before, she might have had enough left over to soothe today's hunger. And with less light to hunt by, it took Fox much longer to find even mice.

Now it was very late and Fox had found only a few mice. She was still very hungry and night was almost over. Mice made a poor winter diet and her thoughts turned to the fat chickens in the henhouse on the farm. Sitting in the snow, she also thought of Jim, Jim's Man, and his gun.

Finally, the compelling bite of hunger drove Fox to the farm.

She moved as quietly as a shadow around the barn-yard. The moon had faded and the wind lay still on the flatlands. Fox moved two steps and froze, listening for every sound, testing the air for every scent. Two steps more, stop, listen, smell. Two steps. Stop. Two steps. Stop.

It took Fox a long time to get to the crack in the barn wall big enough for her to get through. She stopped outside it and stood quivering for long minutes, listening to the farm animals, scenting their animal smells. They didn't smell at all like wild animals. Their scent was sweeter, milder somehow. Over everything was Jim. She didn't know him as Jim, only as dog, but his scent was the one that made her quiver with fear. She could hear his breathing through all of the other sleeping animal sounds. It was heavy and relaxed and she knew he was sleeping. She also knew that he would awake at the smallest unusual sound, or if the wind suddenly stirred and carried her wild scent to his nose.

Fox smelled the fresh, mild scent of a newborn lamb, but it was coming from very near where Jim's scent was. After several more nervous minutes, she crept away toward the henhouse. Two steps. Stop. Two steps. Stop.

The peculiar ruffling sound of sleeping chickens filled her ears as Fox crawled under the henhouse. Her nose was filled with the sharp tang of droppings that had fallen through the cracks in the floor. She didn't like it when one of her senses was overpowered, but she trusted her ears now that her nose was full of chicken smell.

She eased herself up through the crack in the floor she'd used before, and stalked a fat hen on the nest nearest to her. In a flash she had the hen by the neck, hot chicken blood surging into her mouth.

The hen didn't die fast enough. It clucked and flapped and the noise roused the rest of the flock. They set up a horrible racket that overpowered Fox's ears, too. She dragged the dying hen through the crack in the floor and wriggled out from under the henhouse.

Jim was chasing the fox through his dream when the noise from the henhouse startled him. He exploded to his feet and charged into the barnyard before he was fully awake. The wildness of fox filled his nostrils. He lifted his head and scented the air. It came from beyond the henhouse. Jim was off in a flash, baying on the scent trail Fox left behind.

Fox knew she was in trouble even before she heard Jim's trail cry. She knew the chicken noise would awaken him, so she trotted off with the chicken in a direction different from the one that would carry her home. She knew she could not lead Jim to her den. If he found where she lived, she would have no peace.

Fox made her way quickly across the field back of the henhouse. She could hear Jim baying behind, but she took the time to circle twice to try and throw him off her trail. Maybe he would follow the circles around and around without realizing his mistake.

Her last circle took her beside the stream on the far side of the field. She closed her jaws tight on the dead hen and leaped as far as she could onto the ice. She slid a long way when she landed and almost dropped her dinner.

She hoped that the frozen water wouldn't hold

her scent as long as the field and that by the time Jim found it she'd be long gone. She dashed far down the ice-covered stream and jumped back onto the bank. Looping and circling and wriggling through thickets, she made her trail as hard to follow as she knew how.

Fox was so excited by the hunt, and Jim's pursuit, and fear, that she didn't notice the dead hen was dripping blood every so often all along her trail.

Jim noticed it right away. He followed the mixed fox and hen scent. When the fox scent would fade, he would cast about, coal black nose low to the ground, running back and forth until he found another drop of chicken blood. This took Jim a long time, but he kept after the fox even after his feet went numb with the cold and the sun had risen high in the morning sky.

Fox lay snug in her den. She had eaten her fill of the hen, and hidden what was left in a deep wild raspberry thicket. She had licked herself clean of hen's blood, 2 1 picked every speck of ice and snow from her feet, and was curled up waiting for sleep.

She'd been ready for sleep for a long time, but sleep wouldn't come. Her nerves were raw and she couldn't relax. She kept trying to think of other ways she could have thrown Jim off her track. When she couldn't think of any more, she lay quietly and worried.

Jim was nearly worn out by the time he had followed Fox's trail to the hidden valley. Her scent had been stronger since the place in the thicket where he'd found the hen's remains. From there on, Jim's growing excitement of closing in on the fox overpowered his fatigue and cold feet.

Nose close to the ground, Jim followed Fox's scent right up to the honeysuckle vines. From there it was a short jump to the opening of her den. Almost wild with excitement, Jim began to dig furiously at the frozen hard-packed earth around the den entrance.

Fox heard Jim coming before he began ripping at her entryway, but too late to run. She backed into her den as far as she could, trembling with fear and anger, the hair along her spine standing and ruffled. She growled a warning.

Jim heard Fox growl from deep inside her den. The tunnel of frozen earth made the growl seem deeper, louder, more menacing. It also raised Jim's will to fight. He dug faster, harder.

Fighting her fear, Fox wriggled down the passageway toward the entrance to her den.

Jim's nose was full of fox scent and his ears were filled with the sounds of his digging, so he didn't hear Fox creeping toward him. He stopped digging and thrust his muzzle into the opening to see if he could fit.

Fox saw Jim's muzzle and how his lips curled back from his teeth as he growled and tried to force his way into the den. Instinctively, she sprang forward, set her feet, and sank her needle-sharp teeth into Jim's nose.

Jim felt the terrible pain. He shook his head to try

and get loose. He pulled hard, but the pain was too great. He howled and tears came to his eyes.

Fox bounced around the tunnel as Jim shook his head, but she didn't let go. She held fast while he howled and she held fast while he was still and just whined.

After a long time, Fox's jaws ached from holding on to Jim's nose. Her mouth was caked with dry dog blood. She felt weak and a little sick.

Jim's nose hurt like nothing ever hurt him before. All he wanted to do was get free and hold his sore muzzle in the soothing, cool snow. His feet were frozen. His tail was numb. He had to get away, get back to his Man, get help.

Fox couldn't stand it any longer. Maybe dying wouldn't be as bad as this. With great effort she opened her cramped jaws and released Jim's nose.

Jim yelped and pulled his nose out of the hole. He turned and ran for home.

Fox was exhausted, but she knew she had to leave her den. The farm dog knew where she lived and would bring his Man now. But Fox was so tired. She needed to sleep.

Jim's nose still throbbed, but he was coming back up the hill. After his Man had gotten his gun, he urged Jim back to the hunt. Jim brought him right to the valley.

Jim heard his Man cock the gun. He ran up the hillside to Fox's den. He began digging again. Now the fox would die. Jim's Man would kill her.

Under the wild raspberry thicket, Fox finished the last of the hen she'd taken from the farm. Food made her feel better, stronger. She would have a long way to go before she could feel safe enough to dig another den.

She picked herself up and started trotting in the direction of the fading sun. As she went, she remembered her struggle with Jim and growled softly.

It was the defiant growl of a survivor.

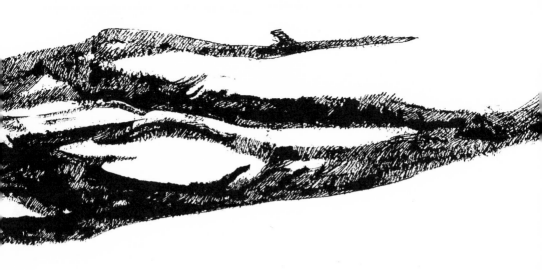

MISSING
LYNX

The bleak light rode low in the granite sky behind its filter of dirty woolen clouds. The depths of winter weighed heavy and held the sun's zenith to a point just cresting the skeletal trees. It had been a long time since warmth had flooded the high country, and the length of the season could be measured in the depth of the snow that quietly strangled activity at this altitude.

Lynx sat, still and silent as death, in the center of a circle of ruffled snow at the foot of a towering spruce. When he glanced about, stray shafts of sunlight struck fire in his angry yellow eyes. Lynx was unhappy still to be out. The hunt he'd begun hours ago under the safe cover of darkness should have been completed before sunrise. Now, he was hungry and caught under the low-sweeping spruce boughs instead of sleeping full bellied in his lair. He felt exposed and vulnerable.

Night belonged to Lynx. It was his element. His blood carried the heritage of the best of his ancestors, the natural traits that made Lynx stronger and better suited to his life and its conditions than even his father or his father's father. The lynx ancestors whose eyes were not as sharp, whose tufted ears were not as keen, whose noses were not as sensitive, whose valuable coats were not as thick, whose soft furred feet were not as big or as silent, whose fangs and claws were not as long and sharp, had failed the test of survival before they could weaken the bloodline.

Lynx moved through the dark forest with the speed, agility, and confidence that allowed him to ambush deer in their beds and sink his fangs deep through their skulls before they could even rise to their feet. His skills brought death so suddenly to the sleeping grouse that they died unconscious of their own plight. Ptarmigan, Lynx plucked from the air before their frantic wing beats could carry them above his savage leap.

Only the elk, the wolf, the puma, and the wolverine were safe from Lynx; he knew their size and power set them beyond his skills. But all the other creatures in his range were prey to Lynx, and he had slain and fed on them all, from the smallest mouse to the fattest mule deer.

Night was his ally, his companion in the hunt. When the creatures of the day retreated to their beds, Lynx left his. Stalking the wary made unwary by sleep, Lynx ruled the dark forest. By day, the puma or wolf pack would struggle to bring down its prey, forced by the light to battle senses tuned for flight and strength doubled by fear. By night, Lynx fell upon his prey and ended its struggle before it could even begin. He bore scars of hurts suffered during a rare botched ambush, but no lingering injuries that would hamper his ability to hunt and force him out of the high country to the sheep pens and chicken houses of the farms in the valley below.

The frailties brought on by age had forced the female puma, who used to range his territory, down to the valley to prey on the livestock there. She had gone last winter and never returned. Livestock was easy prey, but sudden death lived in the houses next to the barns and pens.

Lynx had been down into the valley. He was stalking the henhouse on the uppermost farm when a black devil twice his size exploded from the barn with a deafening roar that put him to flight. A Man appeared seconds later and sent buckshot after him, too. Lynx wanted no part of the farm dogs and their Men, so he avoided the valley ever after.

The high country with its crisp, clear air was his home. Up high there was no wood smoke, no gasoline fumes, no Man smell to dull his nose. There were no farm dogs or buckshot to threaten him. There were no fence lines to cross or naked fields without cover. No barns or henhouses to be trapped in. No muck and mud of civilization. Lynx could live the way he was intended to live, free and wild and by his own wits. He knew the dangers of the puma, the wolf, the wolverine, of falls, and landslides, and fast water. The dangers he faced in the high country were of nature, not of Mankind, and he knew what to do to protect himself.

But his world was now askew. It had tilted when he wasn't aware. He had missed the change somehow. It angered him almost as much as being caught out in the daylight.

His throat vibrated with a low, unconscious rumble of frustration. He lowered his head and licked the two outermost toes on his big left foot. His rough warm tongue soothed his toes a little, but the taste of his own blood mixed with that of cold iron angered him. He 3 1 jumped to the right, away from the taste, and was pulled down at the edge of the circle of ruffled snow.

He landed awkwardly, pulled off balance by the forgotten tether. What kind of animal was it that bit so hard and held so tight for so long? What kind of animal lay silent beneath the snow to jump and bite as you passed by in the night? What kind of animal was so cold and hard that it broke your teeth when you tried to fight it? What kind of animal was so small, yet so strong that you couldn't break free of it? What kind of animal could hurt you so much but that you couldn't hurt back?

Lynx sat up at the edge of the circle of ruffled snow and backed away from the animal that held him by the two broken toes of his left front paw. He backed away until his left leg was stretched tight in front of him, pointing to the center of the circle of ruffled snow. He jerked back hard and the dull throb in his toes turned fang sharp and shrieked up his leg like lightening.

The pain frightened and enraged Lynx and he jumped and flailed and wrestled and screamed against the thing that held him. He bit at the cold iron until his teeth ached and his broken fang screeched for him to stop.

Lynx limped to the center of his circle of snow, dragging his captor with him. He lay down and used his tongue to soothe his mangled toes. Pain pulsed in his foot with every heartbeat. Hunger churned his belly and thirst burned his throat. He ate some snow to cool his mouth, but a strange heat burned from within. He felt hot and cold and weak and sick. His blood colored the snow under his paw bright cherry red.

Lynx tried to relax and sleep, but instinct kept him alert, wouldn't allow sleep to come as he lay exposed in the cold unforgiving light of day.

Night brought raw, frigid winds from the north that drove a bitter snowstorm into the high country. Lynx sheltered as best he could beneath the laden spruce bough, but the snow drifted in on the biting wind. Ice crystals clung to his whiskers and ear tufts and froze in the fur at the corners of his eyes.

Lynx drifted in and out of a troubled sleeplike state. Never really relaxing, never really sleeping, never really awakening, Lynx felt the gnawing of a second night's hunger and the feverish thirst that left his throat hot and sore. He moved to curl up, but the thing that still bit him felt too heavy to move and the pain that surged through his damaged paw forced him to be perfectly still.

He could no longer feel his mangled toes, just the growing area of pain that now encompassed his entire paw and crept in pulses farther up his leg. Lynx knew that he couldn't go on waiting for this thing to let go, but how could he make it release him? Biting it did no good. He had bitten it and chewed it until his fang broke and his mouth bled. Still it held fast.

Dawn brought clear skies, and the light from the sun brightened, but cast none of its heat as far as the high country. In the spruce above Lynx, a fox squirrel darted across the branches and scolded him simply for being nearby. Lynx, hurt and sick and hungry and dry, could only lift his dull yellow eyes to watch. He was too miserable even to growl. After a little while, the fox squirrel returned to his nest to escape the cold. Lynx lay in the snow too weak to shiver. He pillowed his head on his unhurt front paw and licked his numb nose. The bright red tip of his swollen tongue didn't quite disappear when he closed his mouth. Lynx didn't notice.

A wolverine, watching silently from the deadfall tree nearby, waited patiently.

The Boy trudged miserably against the slope of the hillside. The new snow dragged at each step and the straps of his pack pulled at his shoulders. The .22 Magnum rifle he carried felt heavy in his mittened hand. He grumbled that his father had made him leave the warmth of the house on the flatlands below on such a raw day, just to check the trapline he'd set out three days ago.

There wasn't anything in the nine traps he'd picked up and added to his pack so far, and there wouldn't be anything in the last one. He hated having to come so far just to pick up the empty spring-jaw trap, but he knew his father would count them when he got them back to the barn for oiling. If he didn't have all ten, he'd just be sent back out.

Topping a little rise, the Boy's eye was caught by motion back under the spruce bough where he'd set the last trap. He stopped where he was and slowly brought the rifle to his shoulder. He could see through the telescopic sight that a wolverine was worrying something in the middle of the disturbed snow. A prime pelt would bring needed money at the fur auction.

The Boy eased the safety to the fire position, took a deep breath, centered the cross hairs on the wolverine's neck, and squeezed the trigger.

The rifle shot echoed back from the valley as the wolverine thrashed in the circle of ruffled snow. The Boy worked the rifle's action and fired again. And again. And again.

Perhaps it was because he was tired from the climb, or careless in his anger, but the Boy had not aimed true. When he got to where the wolverine lay, he saw his four shots had spoiled the pelt. He kicked the body aside.

The lynx, whose fur looked to be in prime condition, had already been spoiled by the hungry wolverine. The Boy stepped on the spring arms of the trap to release the mangled paw. It was frozen to one cold iron jaw and he had to cut the broken toes free. He held them in his hand for a moment and pulled the claw sheaths back to examine the fierce hooks beneath. He shivered from the cold, put the trap into his pack and dropped the severed toes. He started back down toward the flatlands.

Lynx's clawed toes fell near the center of the circle of ruffled snow he now shared with the wolverine. Overhead, the fox squirrel quietly watched as the Boy stumbled down the snow-covered slope.

ROAN

He stood alone on a small rise, testing the air for the scent of danger and keeping watch over his dominion. Spring had come late to the high plains, as it always did at this altitude, and the heat from the sun soaked soothingly through his thick winter coat. His tail moved constantly against the first of the biting blackflies, and his roan hide twitched involuntarily across his flanks when they pinched bites out of his rump. The flies were a bother, but he'd grown used to them over the years and now they rarely distracted him from his vigilance.

Below him grazed his harem. Moving slowly, heads down, trusting to his watchfulness, they cropped mouthful after mouthful from the tender, sweet shoots of the new grass. Attentive to feeding, their ears were constantly alert to the warning snort or stamp that would bring their heads up as one. All eyes would fix on Roan as he signaled the route of escape or line of defense against intruders or predators.

He'd chosen this range with instinctive care. A cold, snow-fed stream split the perspective like a slightly bent arrow. There were trees enough for shelter from the cold, pelting rain, and for shade from the blistering sun that was to come in the weeks ahead, but not enough cover to camouflage the close stalk of a hungry puma, ravenous wolf pack, or marauding young stallion. Any threat to his harem could be seen long before action would be required.

He breathed deeply of the dry thin air. His nostrils flared and his deeply muscled breast expanded. The scent of female filled the air, and his withers twitched in response. His range-bred mustang veins pulsed with his Spanish blood and he was driven by instinct to pass the genes on. His forebears had roamed wild since they had been freed from the saddles and spurs of the conquistadors in the sixteenth century.

Now, he was wilder than the most spirited of his ancestors. Nature had seen to that. Mustangs foolish enough to let Men—red, black, or white—within reach had been captured and broken to their will. Mustangs too lazy or dim of wit to keep keen watch over their harems had lost them to males more dominant, or to predators more crafty. The insufficiencies in their genes had died with them under the merciless stroke of fang and claw or the lonely inevitability of time.

He was the pinnacle of his strain, the finest in the progression of refinements wrought by the unflinching 4 1 hand of nature. The steel of the breed is strengthened and tempered by the centuries of testing that work instability out of the design. Like the distillation of precious metal from raw ore, his generation was stronger than his father's, and that of his father's father. His grandsons would be fitter still than he or even his sons. And so works the inexorable hand of nature.

There was a new scent on the wind. Interloper.

Roan nickered softly to the herd. Their heads jerked high. All eyes surveyed the horizon. And there he was, galloping with unbridled male confidence, clearing the stream in a single great leap, closing on Roan's harem in a blur the color of new iron.

Roan stamped his forefoot and blew a warning through his nostrils. The mares saw the stranger's approach and shied. Roan bolted through the harem to cut off his rival's rush.

Each met the other in full stride, breast crashing against breast, necks jerking forward, lips curling back savagely. The interloper faltered at impact and Roan was quick to press his advantage. He lashed out with his forefeet, hooves crashing against his adversary. He sank his teeth into the stranger's neck and brought blood. He reared and struck again with his forefeet. Employing an old trick, he whirled as if to run, bolted a few steps, and—as the interloper got to his feet and gave chase—lashed out with his back hooves and caught his rival full-force under his lower jaw. The strength of the blow was redoubled by the stranger's rush to pursue. He was stunned and dropped to his knees. Roan turned back, slashed again with his front hooves, then backed off two steps.

The interloper struggled to his feet, defeated, and turned to trot off out of danger. Roan nipped his rival's rump and trailed him to the edge of the stream. Satisfied the challenge to his harem was overcome, Roan nickered to the mares, paused for a drink, and then returned to his overlook on the rise.

It was twilight and Roan moved restlessly through his harem. The mares were bedded, but remained awake. Periodically, a nervous snort broke the quiet.

Roan's thick winter coat was ruffled against the chill evening air and against the smell of wolf. It was faint but clear on the light breeze that moved down from the mountain peaks and across the high plain. Roan's ears moved continually as he tried to detect any sound that didn't belong in his domain. His hide twitched with the promise of danger as adrenaline surged through him and brought his breath more rapidly into his lungs. Muscles tight with anticipation, he moved stiffly to change his perspective of the gathering gloom. Gray shadows fooled him into seeing wolves that didn't yet exist and he charged these mirages relentlessly.

A single distant howl electrified Roan's senses. All about him, mares lurched to their feet, yearling foals pressing tight against their sides. An answering howl bunched the herd while Roan circled and stationed himself between the source of the sound and his mares. He stamped and snorted a warning.

The mares moved closer together, the herd instinct stronger now against perceived danger. The yearlings were held beside their mothers and always inside the bunched group.

Shapes began to take form. Gray ghosts loping easily, tirelessly, heads low, tongues lolling comfortably, tails relaxed, paws padding soundlessly over the new spring grass.

The leader was a heavy-shouldered brute with one eye socket empty and scarred, the ear on that side a twisted stump. He bore the scars of many challenges to his leadership, and of many struggles with prey larger than himself. His muzzle was grizzled with the many years passed in the high country that had honed his hunting skills to a razor edge.

The lead wolf paused and scanned the harem. His pack drew to a halt around him. He knew his prey. The young, the weak, the sick, the maimed, the one too frightened to stand safely with the rest. He knew his adversary. Roan, standing alert and watchful ahead of his mares. He was the one to be reckoned with. Surging with strength, pride, and protectiveness. He was the danger.

Roan watched the group, but concentrated on the leader. His was the dominant scent from the pack. His was the confidence Roan sensed most. He was the pure hunter, the head that the body of the pack would follow. He was the danger.

Roan snorted and stamped. He coursed back and forth over the same ten yards in front of his mares. He tuned his senses to the pack's leader. He paused, then charged the lead wolf.

The leader sensed the charge, tensed, and dodged easily when it came. The roan was too much animal to fool with. He had to be avoided. His flashing hooves could kill or cripple, but both meant the same end. Death.

Lead wolf feinted toward Roan and cut around his striking hooves. He was past Roan in a flash of gray, charging the herd. The mares cried out, but stood their ground shoulder to shoulder. The yearlings quivered and pressed against their mothers.

Fear hung heavy in the night air and excited the
pack. They circled the mares in twos and threes,

watching. The wolf leader searched for the mare most likely to bolt. Concentrating on the harem, he was almost run down from behind by Roan. He dashed aside just in time.

Roan concentrated on the leader. If he could drive off the one-eyed predator, he knew the pack would follow. He dogged the leader's steps, trusting his mares to keep together and defend themselves. He dashed this way and that, but always the leader avoided him at the last instant.

The pack kept circling. The mares stayed bunched, moving slightly to keep the closest wolves always in sight. The predators could strike in a flash and drag down one of the yearlings in an instant.

The leader circled. Roan harassed him. The herd held together.

Dodging Roan, the leader raced through the mares, growling and snapping his jaws. One yearling bolted. The leader followed. The mother mare cried out in terror. Roan cut the angle of the chase and bowled the leader over, then turned and reared between the scrambling wolf and the yearling. He struck out with his front hooves, then dashed to the yearling's side. Snorting a warning, he herded the youngster back toward the mares.

Set apart from the herd, Roan and the yearling were cut off by the rest of the pack. Roan stood his ground with the foal quivering near his shoulder. The mother mare neighed. The pack closed in.

Roan stamped his hoof and charged the leader. The yearling followed. The leader dodged. Two of the pack ripped at the yearling's flank. The yearling screamed. Roan whirled and drove the wolves off the yearling.

He stood his ground again, blowing hard through his nostrils, filling his straining lungs. The wolves drew nearer, but Roan had gained ground closer to the mares. He gathered his strength and surged again at the pack's leader. The yearling followed. Roan feinted this time, and struck back with his hind feet. He caught a trailing wolf square in the chest, crushing its ribs and tearing its lungs. The wolf howled with pain and the pack broke from its own fear.

Roan led the yearling closer to the herd.

The wolf leader cut off their path. He teased Roan, staying just out of striking distance while the pack closed in on the yearling. One trailing wolf bit deeply into the yearling's hamstring and almost brought it down. Roan kicked out at the leader, then drove off the attacker. Bleeding, the yearling swayed beside Roan. More ground had been gained.

The mares were stamping restlessly and snorting with fear. The yearling's mother nickered to her foal. The smell of blood enraged the herd and spurred the pack.

Roan charged again. Three wolves closed in on the yearling and took it from its feet. Teeth slashed at its flanks and hamstrings. The rest of the pack began closing in.

Roan bolted past the wolves, past the leader, toward his harem. The one-eyed wolf sensed the kill was near and moved for his share. Roan burst into the mares, circled, and raced back to the wolves. The mares followed. The thunder of their hooves split the air.

They were on the pack in an instant. Hooves slashed the air and struck gray heads.

The leader cried out as he suffered a glancing blow. He jumped away and found himself surrounded by surging mares. He retreated from the herd and barked for his pack. Defeated, they followed him across the high plain, tails tucked under, on the run in search of less fearsome prey.

Roan sped their retreat with a final charge, then returned to his mares. One wolf, crippled by a blow that had broken its lower spine, snarled with rage and hurt as Roan approached. Dragging itself by its front paws, it snapped its jaws savagely.

Roan reared and ended its life. Roan knew no compassion, but on rare occasions mercy is the incidental companion of wild instinct. The yearling pressed against its mother who licked the gaping wound above its hock. The yearling trembled with pain and injury and fear.

Roan trotted back to his mares and nosed the yearling. The smell of blood was fierce, but the yearling was alive. The wound was deep, but given time it could heal. Given time, the yearling could grow up. Given time, it could survive.

Half a mile away, the lead wolf paused, lifted his muzzle and filled the night air with the sound of the hunt.

PUMA

Life was hard, as near to the tree line as she lived and hunted. And when winter blew full force against the unprotected cliffs where she made her den, the gales, snow, and frigid temperatures made her bones ache and her joints creak with the cumulative strain of over twenty years of roaming the unforgiving land.

There was a time when winter was just another season to pass, another unfelt tilting of her world. Her fur would grow thick and warm, and she would employ stalking techniques better suited to hunting on snow than on the rustly carpet of the autumn woods. Instinctively, she would spend more time deep in her den, sheltering out of the brunt of the cold, and less time trying to warm herself in the pale rays of the season's feeble sun. Winter didn't threaten her existence, merely altered it as she adapted to the different demands it made on her. And often it was the time when she felt new life stirring deep within her, new life that she would bear in the spring. Like her prey, indeed even like the trees and flowers and grasses of the high country, she would renew her kind with the thaw.

But now, this late in her life, winter weighed heavily upon her like a cloak she couldn't shed. It became a grim burden that bore relentlessly on her existence and reminded her, painfully, of every misstep, tumble, or injury she had sustained in the past. There were days when the hunger that filled her empty belly was easier to bear than the aches that came when she tried to stir from her bed.

Pain was her prime enemy now, confining her and limiting her ability to hunt. The hares and ground squirrels and marmots that had been easy, almost effortless prey in years gone by were now her main diet. Often, even these small creatures could elude her with the speed and agility that were no longer hers.

Stealth was her only ally, but her ability to spring from ambush was ever more rapidly eroding. With the added stiffness brought on by the cold, there were more and more times when her body simply could not carry out the commands her brain issued. There were times when she wanted to spring, when her mind told her limbs to propel her forward, but they would not respond the way she needed them to in order to hunt effectively. More and more often on the days when she could leave her den and hunt, she would return hungry and exhausted. Slowly, she became a gaunt, desperate shadow of the magnificent creature she had once been.

Hunger drove her from the den where she had shivered through two days and a night, weathering out a big blow from the north. The new day dawned crisp and bright and clear with a promise of warmth that went unfulfilled. Her only respite from the misery of the storm was the calm that followed it. The raw northern winds that had carried in the snow had blown themselves out with the effort. The air this day hung dead still about the cliffs and crags she prowled.

She spent an hour silently stalking a lone marmot, only to have it bolt from under her outstretched claws into a cleft in the rock. It left behind three bright tantalizing drops of blood that glared on the new snow and teased her sense of smell. She ran her tongue across them and swallowed the frozen hint of nourishment. Her stomach growled in empty protest.

She spent another hour creeping cautiously toward a
noisy group of ground squirrels scolding each other as

they foraged among the rocks. As she readied her rush, a lone sentinel spied her hunched form and barked a warning that sent the group to cover before she could pounce.

She walked her territory with patient urgency. She paused to watch a group of mountain goats several hundred yards up the mountain but passed them by, knowing she had neither the energy nor dexterity to bring one down. She came across a grouse napping high above her in the boughs of an evergreen and knew instinctively that she had no chance at it. By the time the sun reached its zenith for the day she knew it was time to abandon her hunt in the high country. If she were to eat today, it wouldn't be the quick, cautious game of her normal range.

Hunger drove her down from the relative safety of the high country. It drove her down to the foothills overlooking the flats below. It drove her to the upper pastures of the farm.

She settled wearily on her stiff haunches as the last

rays of the sun faded behind the peaks above her. Her ears twitched as they captured the animal sounds, and pricked forward to the sharper, more careless, often metallic sounds made by the Man and the Boy as they hurried to finish their chores in the dying light. Her nostrils quivered with the scent of the beasts that crowded the feed troughs in the pens and outbuildings below.

Sweeter, stranger smells lay under the pungence of the barnyard; wood smoke, human sweat, cooked food—and the scent of dog. Dog triggered the instinctive response that raised the fur along Puma's spine and down her tail. Alert to the slightest change in sight, sound, or smell, she felt her throat quiver with the low rumbling of a warning growl. Her claws twitched slightly inside their living sheaths. In the buildings below her lay animals grown fat and lazy and stupid and weak over their generations of domestication. Below her too lay the danger she must risk for the food she required.

Her senses grew raw from the waiting, the waiting

for dark, for quiet, for opportunity, for nourishment. Her body grew raw from the cold.

Finally, finally she lay just inside the fence bordering the sheep shanty. She rested for a while, gathering her dwindling strength, concentrating her will for the final rush. She watched the unknowing sheep settle, one by one, into sleep.

Her joints creaked silently as she rose, and shrieked soundlessly as she pushed herself into the stalking crouch. With infinite care she placed each paw softly in front of the other. She felt the minute squeaks more than heard them as her weight depressed the dry snow. Long minutes passed as she worked herself into position.

Her strike was like a sudden thunderclap to the sheep. It came without warning and momentarily froze the instantly awake flock. In the split second it took them to react, she broke the neck of a young lamb and quick-stepped out of the shanty, carrying her prey. The kill was too quick for the lamb to even make a sound. The puma left behind only her scent and the smell of   5 9 death, but it was enough to set the flock in terrified motion.

Inside the farmhouse the noise from the sheep shanty roused the farm dog from sleep. Hound-bred nostrils picked up the scent of big cat. The dog barked a continuous warning that awakened the Man. The Man rushed to his upstairs window and opened the sash in time to see the puma fading into the deeper darkness outside the barnyard. He knew he was too late to do anything about the big cat, but he went downstairs to calm the dog.

Puma lay in her temporary lair in the lee of a deadfall surrounded by the scant remains of her meal. There was little she hadn't consumed—wool, skull, large bones cracked and licked clean of marrow, a few splashes of blood—and her hunger was quieted for the night. She curled into a tight circle, pillowed her head on her front paws, and fell asleep.

Twice during the night she had been awakened by her aching joints and had stretched awkwardly and changed position, trying to find some relief and return to her rest. Sleep came more slowly each time, and when the sun rose she arose with it.

The lamb had been enough last night to allow sleep, but her hunger returned with the new day. It was another ache to add to the others that filled her being as she moved about beyond the upper reaches of the farm. She walked stiffly at first, overcoming the effects of the numbing cold and the night's inactivity. She felt her joints slowly loosening and her muscles warming slightly with the movement, but it was miles before she moved with any hint of the grace she had once possessed.

She made a meager breakfast of a nest of mice she discovered near the tree line, trapping them under her front paws and swallowing each one whole after a single crunching bite. They were better than nothing, but even a double paw-full of mice did little to quiet her stomach.

Often, she would turn her head to look down over the flats and inhale deeply the promising scent of the barnyard. Last night's lamb had been far easier to take than she could have imagined. The dog that she'd smelled had erupted in furious voice once the sheep had aroused it, yet she saw nothing of it. There was no pursuit, no chase. Dog on the loose was something to fear, but this one seemed confined to the house with the Man. Perhaps, if she found nothing better than mice during the day, she would return with the darkness to the farm and try for a larger lamb that would make more than a single meal.

She passed the day without finding prey, save for the few morning mice. As the sun faded, hunger again drove her down from the hills to the farm. Again she waited for the sounds of the Man and the animals to settle toward sleep. Again she made her painful stalk to just outside the sheep shanty. Again she lay and collected herself for what she needed to do.

Silently she rose and began making her way to the shanty. The deep sounds of heavy breathing filled her ears and told her the flock was asleep. The dense smells of the barn and shanty excited her with the promise of a second easy kill. Even the sharp chill of the winter night lay lighter upon her.

Closing the distance to the shanty door, she stepped silently on the frozen threshold. Dozens of sleeping sheep crowded the interior. Her eyes fell on a lamb of the proper size and age to provide meat for more than one meal without being too large to kill instantly and carry off easily.

She crouched to spring, when suddenly the farm-house door banged behind her. The sound startled her and she leaped forward among the sheep defensively. The door to the shanty was blocked by the milling sheep and the farm dog. Sheep sounds and barking split the night. Instinctively, she retreated to the far corner of the shanty where the angle of the walls protected her back from attack. Once there, she turned to face the dog across the expanse of sheep.

The farm dog maintained his place at the only door to the shanty, barking and growling, keeping the sheep from bursting out. Fearful of the dog and the cat, the 63 sheep finally settled into a nervous, twitching clump crowded against one wall as far away from both animals as they could manage to be.

The puma measured her antagonist. The farm dog was a large muscular brute with bright sturdy fangs and the energy of an animal in its prime. The years had blunted her teeth along with her physical skills. She looked about, seeking an avenue of escape. There was only the door. She gauged the distance and her chance of bursting by the dog in a sudden rush. She tensed her muscles and felt the pain once again wash over her. In the span of a heartbeat she knew, finally, she was too frail.

She flinched at the metallic clicks as the farmer, who stepped now into the doorway beside the dog, thumbed back the hammers on the shotgun.

Mercifully, she never heard the blast.

LONE WOLF Alone.

For the first time in his life, he was truly alone. He lay out of the wind in the shelter of a small depression on the high plain, filling his nostrils with the fading scent of his pack. He could barely pick out the dominant smell of two or three individuals, but the spoor of the others had weakened to the point where he mostly smelled just wolf. If the pack had been traveling with the wind instead of into it, even those lingering scents would have faded beyond recognition.

He licked the back of his forepaw and rubbed the wet spot soothingly over the sunken socket of his left eye. Injured years ago during the struggle that had gained him leadership of the pack, the ruined eye often weeped and troubled him even though it had healed without infection. His left ear, bitten to a twisted stump in the same confrontation, bothered him little except when the freezing winds blew out of the north.

New aches added to his discomfort. His shoulder pulsed with pain from the glancing hoof blow of the roan stallion that had driven him off a try at a yearling mustang. The roan had fought well and routed the pack, injuring some, killing others.

The bruised shoulder would heal, but the conflict with the wild horses had cost him more than a missed meal. His lack of success had encouraged the large black male to challenge his leadership of the pack.

Not far from the mustang herd, the challenger had begun dogging his tracks, then pacing by his blind side. Ignored by the one-eyed leader, the challenger became brazen and began bumping the leader's shoulder. When he could avoid conflict no longer, the leader turned suddenly and bulled over the challenger, knocking him off his feet. Youthful strength and re-flexes brought the challenger back in a flash and the battle was on in earnest.

The challenger circled to the leader's blind side, taking advantage of the weakness. Time and again he would feint a rush and then sweep to the sightless flank. The leader guarded well against this tactic, but his injured shoulder and the effort against the mustangs had made demands on his strength that began to show. His reactions slowed enough for the challenger to leap in, sink his fangs into the leader's flank or haunch, then retreat before the leader could retaliate effectively.

Conserving his dwindling strength, the leader stood his ground and waited for his adversary to come to him. No effort was wasted chasing the younger animal. He met each rush with bared fangs and snapping jaws. Experience favored the leader early and he was able to return the challenger's bites with his own, but he was lucky now to strike true a third of the time.

His tongue lolled over his bared fangs and his chest heaved with exertion. Unwilling to surrender, his confidence began to erode with his strength. It had been years since a challenge to his leadership had brought fear to his heart, but he felt it now. He was tired and hurt and half blind, while the challenger was fit and strong and whole. Suddenly he was unsure of his invincibility.

Instinct told him the key to the battle was to disable the challenger quickly, before his remaining strength left him. As the challenger began his next feint, the leader suddenly surged to meet him. He went for the challenger's front leg, knowing a full-effort bite could break it and win the fight.

His teeth closed on skin and fur as the challenger proved too quick for the crushing full-leg bite. The leader pulled back on the mouthful, trying to unbalance the challenger, but the younger wolf turned into him instead of retreating. The leader felt the sharp fangs of his rival sink into the thick muscles along the back of his grizzled neck. He released the leg hold to howl with pain.

The challenger reared on his hind legs, pulling the leader with him, and shook his head violently back and forth. The leader felt the fangs go deeper into his neck and the muscles begin to tear. It was the end; if he resisted, the younger wolf would kill him. Only one thing could save him now. Instinctively he forced the aggression from his body and went limp.

Sensing his advantage, the challenger shook the leader once more, then released him. The defeated leader dropped to the ground and the young victor stood over him, growling menacingly. Any sign except submission would mean the older wolf's death as the pack shifted its loyalty and closed in around him. He whimpered and rolled onto his back with his tail drawn up between his legs. Rolling his head back, the older wolf offered his throat to the new leader as the sign of ultimate defeat and submission. The younger wolf walked away stiff-legged, the fur on his back ruffled with animal pride.

Other young males closed in on the old wolf, fangs bared, throats rumbling. They surrounded him and nipped him in a hundred places, driving him from their midst. No longer a member of the hierarchy, the rest of the pack treated him like an enemy and tormented him until he loped, limping, off by himself.

He found the sheltered depression in the high plains and watched as the new leader took his place at the head of the pack and led it off in search of prey. The defeated wolf watched until the pack disappeared over a slight rise, then relied on his nose to follow the fading scent drifting back on the wind.

Slowly, cautiously, because of the pain that lanced through his neck muscles at the slightest move, the one-eyed wolf began to soothe the tears and bites that reddened so many places on his grizzled hide. Already the stiffness that followed injury began to set in. He was hungry and thirsty, but too hurt to search for either water or food.

Given a little quiet time and moderate weather, he could heal and begin what was to be a solitary journey through the rest of his life. Given a little luck in finding food and water without having to expend too much effort he could pull through, as he had after losing his eye so many years ago.

Given time. Given luck.

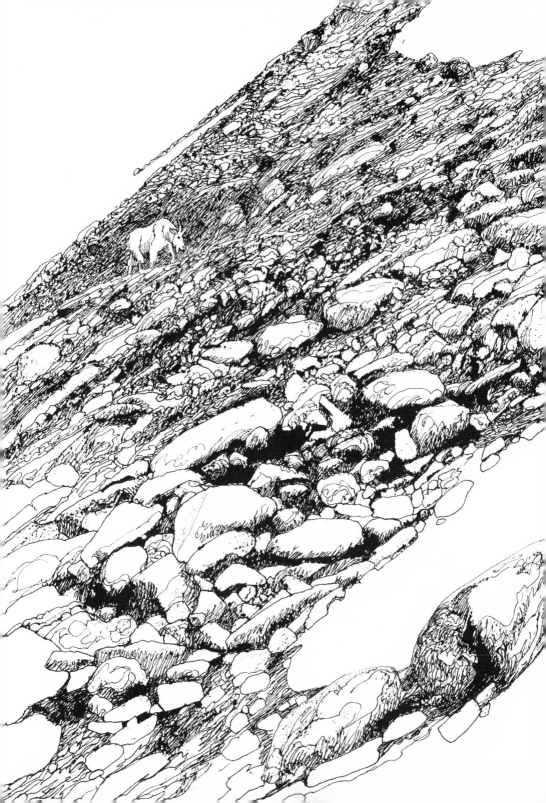

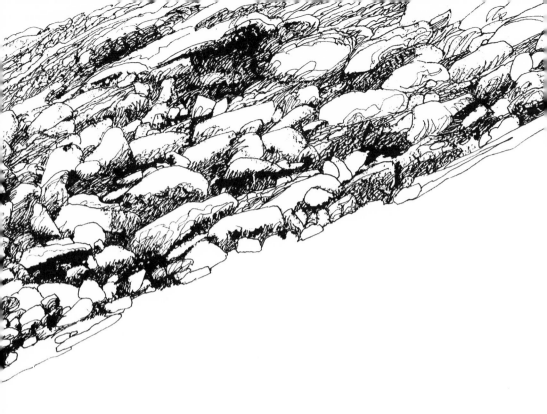

NANNY

She was in pain, too much pain to take another step. She stood for a moment on an outcrop along the narrow, windswept trail high up on the mostly scree covered, treeless windward face. The pain surged and tied her belly in knots. Carefully, because of the pain and her precarious location, she settled to her knees and then onto her swollen belly. She leaned slightly to the uphill side of the slope to ease the pressure on the center of her hurt, and cast watchful eyes over the terrain for signs of danger. Her wet black nostrils flared as she tested the wind for any scent of predators. Her ears flicked alertly back and forth, but the only howl she heard was that of the north wind. Her nearly silent moan was carried away and lost as it was driven before the cold blast. Clouds the color of graphite hurtled toward the peaks above her and drowned the brilliant afternoon sun.

May was bright and warm and green down on the flatlands, but two miles above sea level winter was challenging spring for dominance of the rugged landscape. Dangerous weather could still roll in this late in the season and catch the unwary in its deadly embrace. There was plenty of snow left on the crags, and the gathering dark clouds held the promise of more yet to come.

She'd felt uneasy since early morning when her extended family group began moving along the radical inclines of the mountainside, foraging for the lichens and tender young fir they favored. She'd fallen behind the group almost from the start, but had managed to catch up when many of the other nanny goats and their yearlings stopped at a limestone mineral lick. She rested while the others satisfied their natural craving for salt, and she moved off with the first to leave. Even so, by midday the family had wandered far ahead and she fell farther and farther back until the last straggler ahead of her had disappeared among the treacherous twistings of the trail.

Scenting the change in the weather, she'd struggled to move faster, but the weight in her belly sapped her strength and her altered balance made her pay closer attention to where she placed her horny-edged, spongy-centered hooves. A slip at this height, on a trail this difficult, could easily kill. There was nothing to break a fall or slow the pull of gravity before she would plummet onto the jagged outcrops far below.

Her dark eyes narrowed against the shrieking wind and the growing coil of pain. She shifted her bulk   77 nervously, carefully. The hurt subsided and she breathed more easily. When her insides knotted she panted shallowly, then held her breath during the worst of it. Time and again the pain would flood over her, subside, then return in a growing tide. The periods of rest between grew briefer and briefer, the hurting times longer and longer. She was confused by what was happening to her, but curiously unafraid. Losing sight of her family group distressed her more than the episodes of pain.

She knew that she was vulnerable in her aloneness. It was always the member of the group caught alone, cut off from the gathered strength of many, who fell prey to the roving puma, the savage wolverine, the eagle who struck from above, or the coyotes who drained their quarry's strength with relentless pursuit. To be found alone meant almost certain death.

The weight in her belly shifted and a warm dampness spread beneath her hind legs. It warmed and then chilled her as the north wind drove away the heat and began to freeze the liquid to her thick, shaggy pelt. She squirmed a bit to drier ground and clenched herself as her belly constricted. Moisture, almost like tears, dropped from her eyes and froze on her long, soft, protective eyelashes.

When the pain subsided she again scanned the slopes for any hint of danger. A soft scrabbling sound drew her attention to a ground squirrel who was scurrying toward a den opening between some rocks directly above her. The little rodent's movement kicked loose some scree which gained momentum on the slope and rained down on her. She remained still. When the squirrel disappeared between the rocks she surveyed the terrain and found it deserted.

As the pain returned, the first large, heavy flakes of snow began to fall on her.

By early afternoon the pain was nearly constant. The snow was falling steadily and covered the ground around her. It lay lightly on her thick wool, but didn't reach her skin. The cold froze her moist breath into a slight, crystallized beard. She shifted position awkwardly because of the pain. Her belly strained and constricted to expel its burden of new life. She felt the pressure between her legs and her breath came in hurried gasps.

She nosed the still wet kid. It lay with its legs curled under, blinking at the unexpected brightness of the half dark. She prodded her newborn offspring to its feet and stood, tired and patient, while it nursed a while in the middle of the storm. The kid was still unsure of its feet and shifted constantly to keep its balance. With every minute that passed it became stronger and more confident.

The storm gathered intensity as mother and kid made their way slowly up the treacherous trail. The combined effects of the storm made travel difficult. Heavy clouds reduced the sun's light, while falling snow fogged vision. The snow already on the ground obscured foot traps and loose rocks. Every uncertain step threatened their lives.

Driven by the herd instinct, she kept a pace slow
enough to allow her kid to keep up. Every few minutes

she paused to allow the newborn to rest. Often during these stops, the kid nursed quietly.

Gradually the snow built up on the trail until the kid could travel only in the path left by its mother's footsteps. She plowed on, clearing the way upward. She was nearly exhausted from the exertion of giving birth, but she was driven to rejoin the herd. Behind her the newborn kid fought against the buffeting wind, struggling on through the falling snow.

She stopped instantly when she heard the bleat. She turned carefully and found the kid kneeling in the tracks she'd made. It bleated again and settled onto its belly. She moved to stand over it and bent her head to nudge its neck reassuringly. She sheltered the small body from the storm as best she could and waited. The kid closed its eyes.

After a while she nosed her newborn awake. She licked its face, urged it to its feet, and encouraged it to nurse. Rested a bit, the kid nudged her belly energetically. When she grew tired of waiting, she stepped carefully over her young and moved off up the slope. The kid followed.

Up ahead a rock slide blocked the path. It was covered with snow, but the rough scrabble was unfrozen and dangerously loose. She moved up cautiously to cross it.

Her weight caused the mounded scree to shift and her footing gave way. She scrambled instinctively against the sliding rocks. Adrenaline fed new strength to strained muscles. As the tumbling mass rolled off down the slope, her hooves found solid ground. She gathered herself and looked for her kid. It stood alone on the far side of the slide. It bleated and stepped forward onto the loose stones. At the first sign of movement underfoot, the kid jumped back.

She baaed encouragingly to her newborn and stamped her hoof. It moved forward, then retreated again. She stamped again and blew softly through her nostrils. The kid bleated but didn't move. She stepped forward until the slide threatened to pitch her down
the slope.

Looking around, she moved cautiously uphill. She picked her way around the loose edges of the slide until she was back beside her kid. She licked its face and turned straight back up the slope, avoiding the rockfall completely. She struggled to overcome the combined resistance of deep snow and steeper terrain. Her kid bleated, but she kept going. It had no choice but to follow the rift she left in the snow.

She pressed on, snorting softly to encourage the kid. The newborn struggled against the steep slope, but made progress. Step after step she plowed on. Step after step the kid followed. Gradually the slope began to lessen and, finally, the nanny and her kid reached the end of their exhausting climb.

Just ahead, sheltering out of the worst of the storm behind a soaring granite tower, was her family group. She stopped to nuzzle her newborn kid before leading the way through the deepening snow. Overhead, the wind tore a hole in the clouds and a brilliant shaft of sunlight fell onto the crags.

PATCH

Patch lay quietly on the old braided rug by the woodstove, listening to the winter wind screaming over the mouth of the downspout at the kitchen corner of the farmhouse. Her grayed muzzle was pillowed on her two forepaws and one drawn-up back paw. Her other back leg stuck out stiffly to the side. She whimpered slightly and shifted awkwardly to try and ease the pain she felt in that withered limb.

Winter was hard on Patch. She'd seen many seasons come and go, and she enjoyed the changing aspects of each.

Spring brought fresh earthy scents to enjoy as nature cleared her bosom of the white cloak she'd worn and gently arrayed herself in a new wardrobe of browns and delicate greens. New sounds filled the air as songbirds returned and wild geese passed over the farm to their summer range in the far north. There was plenty for Patch to snuffle with her keen nose and to investigate with her sharp ears, movement to be seen and a new sense of bustle around the farm to enjoy and take part in.

Her favorite spring day was when the men came to shear the sheep. It was her job to keep the flock gathered, racing back and forth, nipping at their rumps and barking. By the end of the day, Patch was exhausted, but her Master always fed her a special dinner and then stroked her neck until she fell asleep.

Summer was Patch's second favorite season. Nature covered most of its brown with deep greenery and showed off the thousand verdant hues in bright spotlights of yellow sunshine. Patch explored her domain, the farm, and spent her time mostly as she pleased. If she found herself at some far corner of the farm when the sun set, there was no need to return to the safety of the house or barn and she spent many a night out, bedded down in a cool grassy nest of her own choosing. During the time of the full moon, Patch investigated the lives of the night creatures and moved freely among them. Often she went fishing with her Master, and she loved to swim the cool green water of the deep hole in the stream at the edge of the upper pasture.

When fall ignited summer's green finery with cool flames of crimson and gold, Patch's blood raced with new excitement. Fall was the time of the hunt, and Patch anticipated the season as anxiously as her Master. She became adept at the tasks he required of her.

She stalked the fence lines and brushwood, searching for the scent of grouse or rabbit. She approached so stealthily that their quarry held tight in the hope that it would be overlooked. Then, at her Master's signal, Patch burst upon the hideaway and gave chase to an explosion of feathers and noise or the quick darting rush of the cottontail.

She nosed through the cornfields of the farm for the sharp scent of pheasant or partridge. Partridge held until flushed, but the wily pheasant often made a run for it, dodging down the rows of harvested stalks. Patch raced after the runner and forced it airborne so her Master could take a clear shot over the obstructing cornstalks.

And there were fine, crisp days late in the season when Patch rode in the truck with her Master to the lake many miles from the farm.

There, in the tall reeds, she lay silently at his feet, waiting for the honking and the distant swish of wings that signaled the wheeling arrival of the wild geese, heading south for the winter. The geese turned in circles over the lake and looked at the rubber decoys Patch's Master had strung as Judas goats on the water. Patch began to shiver with excitement at the first distant sound, and her quivering told her Master to begin playing a deadly siren's song on his goose call.

Seeing deceptive companions floating safely on the water and hearing the feeding calls, the wild geese turned less wary and came gliding in to be met by the patterns of lead shot fired by Patch's Master. Patch watched closely and marked the splashes where the slain fell. Then, at a touch from her Master, she rocketed into the numbing water and struck out powerfully for the fallen. She cradled the still warm body in her soft mouth and tasted the blood they'd drawn together, Patch and her Master. Never ever did she break so much as a feather.

When she found a rare goose that was wounded, but not yet dead, she cradled the struggling form as carefully as she had the others and returned it to her Master for the coup de grace. All she asked was to feel his rough palm on her muzzle and to hear the brief word of reward. Then she shook off the water and returned to his feet to await the next flight.

After the hunt was done, Patch padded wearily back to the warmth of the truck, pillowed her head on her Man's thigh and slept through the journey home.

Winters were always hard on Patch. The activity level on the farm fell to the drudgery of maintenance chores, feeding the flock of sheep and the few cows, keeping after the roofing that often ripped loose during the fierce storms that dipped below the Canadian border and blew in from above the Arctic Circle. There were short trips to town in the truck when Patch had to wait, shivering, for her Master and his wife to return from their errands.

And then there was the winter hunt.

Patch was never allowed to take part in these wintry forays for deer and elk. She learned quickly that the enticing animal smells left by antlered game could only be enjoyed from tracks and trails, never ever to be pursued.

Each winter, there came an evening when Patch's

Master brought out the big rifle that Patch had grown to hate. Then he would rummage in his closet for the bright orange coveralls and heavy boots he wore on his trips high up the mountain. Patch whined and quivered and shadowed her Master, but he would pat her and speak quietly to her and then leave her shut up in the house when he drove off before the sun rose.

She spent the time until he returned, days some-times, pacing and scratching at the door to go out, and scratching at the door to come in, and sleeping small, fitful, dream-filled naps.

But the day always came when he did return, often with the heavy carcass of a mule deer or an elk weighing down the bed of the truck. Patch ran to greet him, yelping like a pup and nipping at his sleeve until he stopped fussing with the kill and fussed over her. He thrust his scratchy chin against her muzzle and whis-pered soothing words into her ear. He stroked under her chin and then grabbed her ruff and shook her until they tumbled, tussling, into the snow. Patch was happy then and content to sit and watch while he hung the carcass in the barn and butchered it. She filled her nose with the wild smell of meat, and of hide, and of death in the high country, and was filled herself with the joy of her Master's return.

Patch was ever faithful, even when her Master brought home a whining, squirming mass of black fur and big feet. He called this intruder Jim and seemed to want Patch to care for it. As soon as she sensed his desire, Patch mothered this Jim with all the love and care his own mother had lavished on him. If that was what Patch's Master desired, she did her best to please him. All she ever asked in return was the feel of his rough palm and the sound of a kind word.

It wasn't too many seasons after Jim's arrival that he joined Patch and her Master in the hunts they used to share alone. Her Man wanted Jim along and Patch suffered his presence grudgingly. She instructed him in his duties and punished his failings to learn with gentle nips and nudges. When he crushed a bird, Patch bullied him off the retrieve and carried it gently back to her Master. When he failed to mark the fall of a goose, she led him to the spot. Then *she* took the bird.

Soon Jim began to hunt nearly as well as Patch and to compete with her for every stand, flush, or retrieve. Before too many more seasons, Jim overshadowed Patch. She barked angrily and nipped at Jim, trying to bully him out of the hunt, but Jim stood fast. Patch resented Jim's youthful strength.

One spring day, as Patch tussled with her Master in the barn, her hind foot slipped into a rat hole gnawed between the flooring planks. She was jumping to catch his sleeve when the strength of her push slid her foot into the hole and wrenched her knee. Patch felt something give way in the joint and she yelped. She pulled hard to free her foot and the effort twisted her damaged limb even more. Something popped, and she cried out again in pain.

Her Master freed her foot, but the damage was done. She spent weeks limping on three feet, then began to put her foot down, cautiously.

She could never trust the limb again. Each time she romped too strongly or tried to run too quickly, the joint betrayed her and sent bolts of pain lancing through her leg.

In time she could do no more than lope gently. Her Master stopped taking her afield and hunted only with Jim.

When Patch could no longer even lope, she went everywhere at a careful shuffle.

Eventually, she stopped using the leg at all and hobbled slowly around the yard, barn, and garden.

This winter season, she was reluctant even to leave the house. She ventured into the yard only to relieve herself. The rest of the time she spent seeking the soothing heat of the stove. She left the kitchen only to join her Man in his room and pillow her head on his slippered feet while he read.

Increasingly Patch avoided the boisterous Jim. Every careless nudge sent gnawing pain through the injured joint. She yelped and snarled and nipped furiously at

Jim, but he was too quick for her to chastise. He simply dodged away and sought quieter places.

Late one evening, at the end of a rare whole day spent alone with her Master in his room, Patch followed his soft encouraging calls to the barn. There, in the light of the kerosene lamp that was so seldom used now that there were electric lights in the barn, Patch watched as her Master took a flannel-wrapped parcel from the big pocket of his hunting jacket.

Patch's Master fed her a strip of elk jerky, her favorite treat, while he unwrapped the blue-steel revolver that had belonged to his father. As Patch chewed on the dried meat, he loaded a single cartridge into the cylinder.

Patch's ears pricked up at the metallic clicks the revolver made when her Master cocked the hammer and brought the cartridge in line with the barrel. Her tail thumped against the old boards of the barn as she felt his rough palm on her head and heard, for the last time, a kind word.